不能错过的 DISNEP 迪士尼 双语经典电影故事

U0660638

DISNEP·PIXAR
迪士尼 皮克斯

INSIDE OUT 头脑特工队

官方完整版

[美] 迪士尼公司 著
谢 沐 译

国家开放大学出版社出版 国开童媒（北京）文化传播有限公司编
北 京

莱莉一出生，乐乐就出现了。乐乐是一个情绪小人。她在掌管莱莉大脑的控制中心——大脑总部里工作。在那里，透过莱莉的眼睛，乐乐可以从眼前的大屏幕上看到这个世界。当莱莉的爸爸妈妈第一次见到女儿时，乐乐也正惊奇地看着他们。

On the day Riley was born, Joy appeared. Joy was an Emotion. She worked inside Headquarters, the main control **center** in Riley's mind. There, on the giant **screen**, Joy could see the world through Riley's eyes. She watched with **wonder** as Riley's parents looked at their daughter for the first time.

乐乐希望莱莉的生活充满欢乐。她的目标就是用快乐的黄色记忆球填满莱莉的大脑总部。乐乐是莱利唯一的情绪小人，她觉得这份工作会一直顺利地进行下去！

Joy wanted Riley's life to burst with happiness. Her goal was to keep cheerful yellow memory **spheres** rolling through Headquarters. And since she was the only Emotion, Joy figured her job was going to be pretty easy!

可是莱莉才出生了三十三秒，另外一个情绪小人就出现了。她的名字叫忧忧。这个小个子的蓝色情绪小人刚一开始操控大脑总部，莱莉就哭了起来。乐乐赶紧把忧忧往旁边推。

But just thirty-three seconds after Riley was born, another Emotion appeared. It was **Sadness**. As the small blue Emotion took the controls in Headquarters, Riley began to cry. Joy quickly pushed Sadness **aside**.

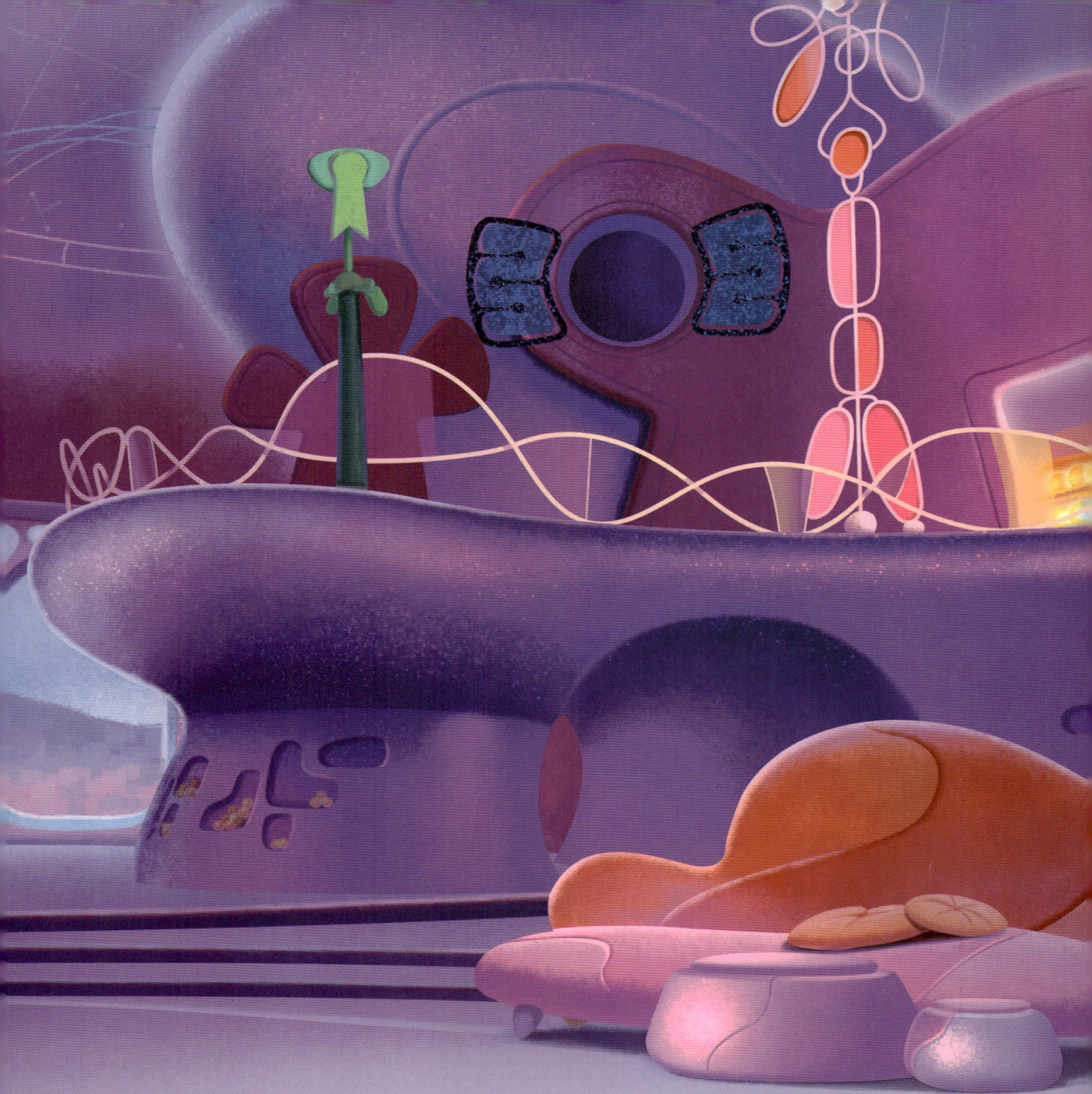

紧接着又有**新的情绪小人**陆续来报到，大脑总部里越来越拥挤了。

　　每个情绪小人都会轮流操作控制台，引导莱莉完成每一天的任务、与别人的交流以及新的挑战。在乐乐看来，每一个情绪小人都很重要。

Headquarters soon became more crowded as **new Emotions** reported for duty. Each one took his or her turn at the **control panel**, and guided Riley through everyday **tasks**, talking to other people, and **challenges**. It seemed to Joy that most of the Emotions had an important purpose.

怕怕负责莱莉的安全。如果莱莉要迈过一条危险的电线，他就会操作控制台引导她安全地迈过去。

Fear kept Riley safe. If there was a dangerous power **cord** to cross, he was the Emotion to safely guide her to the other side.

所有看上去可能让人讨厌的东西都归**厌厌**负责。她帮助莱莉决定是该吃了它，还是该吐掉它！

Anything that was **potentially gross** was handled by **Disgust**. She helped Riley decide whether to accept it . . . or **spit** it out!

怒怒比其他情绪小人更加懂得该怎么处理生活中遇到的不公平。每当莱莉受了委屈，他都会帮助莱莉维护自己，争取公平。

And no one knew how to handle life's injustices better than **Anger**. He helped Riley stand up for herself and demand **fairness**.

可是，说到忧忧……为什么莱莉需要忧忧呢？她好像只会让莱莉不开心，这与乐乐想要给莱利带来欢乐刚好相反。所以，乐乐总是尽可能地让忧忧远离控制台。

But Sadness . . . why did Riley need her? She always seemed to make Riley sad, which was the **opposite** of what Joy wanted. So Joy tried to keep Sadness off the **console** in Headquarters as often as possible.

11

在莱莉的大脑里，总部外面是五个**个性小岛**：家庭岛、诚实岛、冰球岛、友谊岛和淘气岛。

Outside Headquarters in Riley's Mind World were Riley's five **Islands of Personality**: Family, Honesty, Hockey, Friendship, and **Goofball**.

这些个性小岛通过光束桥与大脑总部连接。莱莉经历过的重大时刻都会给她留下深刻的记忆，这些重要的记忆形成了莱莉的核心记忆。它们通过光束桥不断地传送能量，以保证个性小岛的正常运转。

The islands were **connected** to Headquarters by lightlines. Riley's core memories, the super-important memories that came from the biggest moments in her life, sent power through the lightlines to keep the islands running.

在莱莉还是孩子的时候，乐乐常常操纵着控制台，所以莱莉度过了一个快乐的童年。每一天，大脑总部都充满了快乐的黄色记忆球。莱莉十一岁之前，一切都像乐乐计划的一样……可是突然有一天，一切都变了。

With Joy **in charge**, Riley had a great childhood. Every day, yellow memory spheres filled up Headquarters. Riley's first eleven years went just as Joy had **planned** . . . but then everything changed.

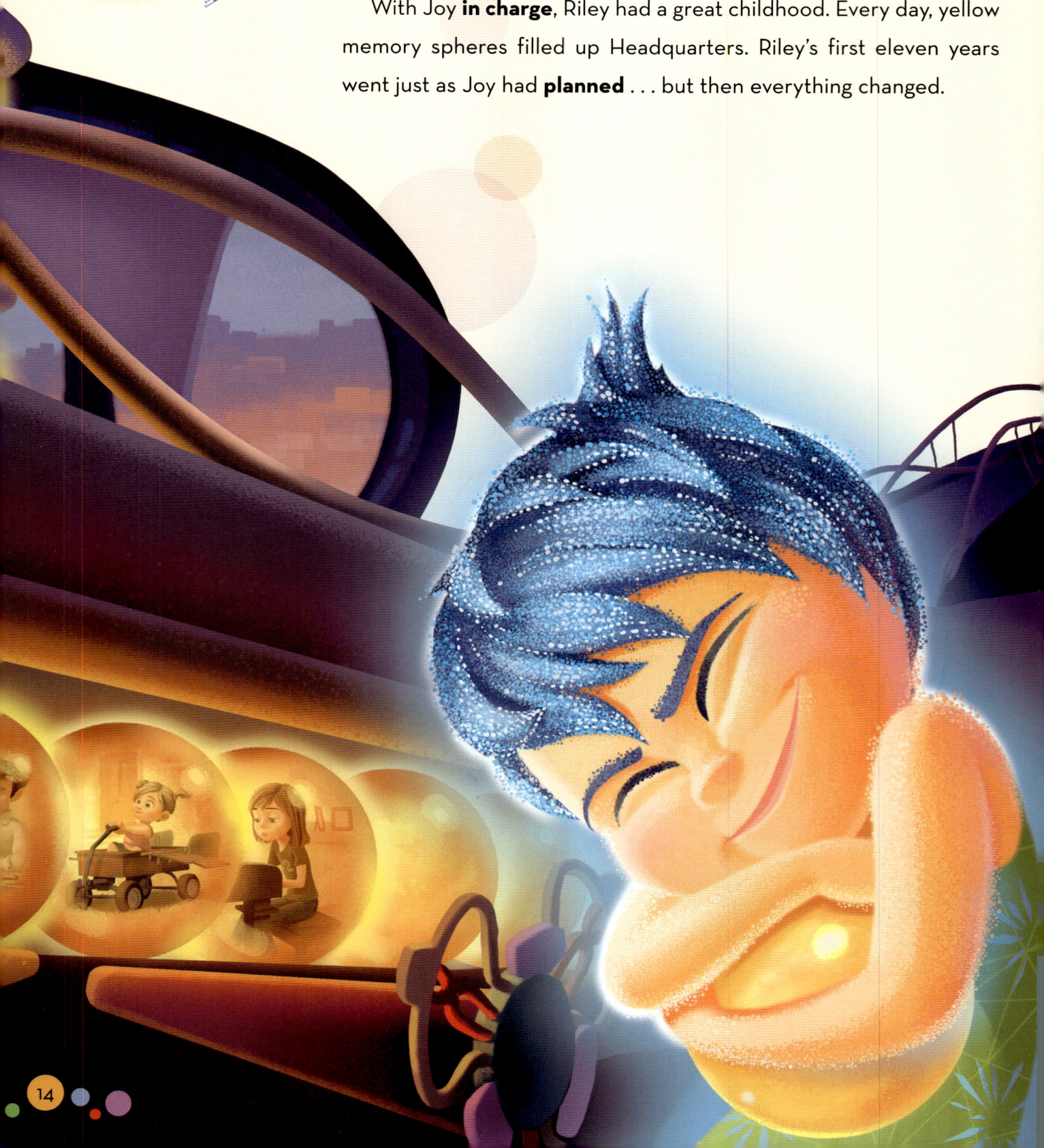

莱莉的父母卖掉了在明尼苏达州的房子，全家人一起搬到了**旧金山**。

Riley's parents sold their house in Minnesota, packed up, and moved the **family** to **San Francisco**!

他们刚到新家的时候，**情绪小人们都感到非常害怕**。这是一栋很小的房子，到处阴森森的，还散发着奇怪的味道。

When they arrived at their new home, **the Emotions were horrified**. The house was small and **spooky**, and it smelled **weird**.

乐乐想让大家都打起精神来。 "我想到了一个好主意！"她一边喊着，一边往控制台里塞进一个灵光一现球。

只见莱莉忽然抓起一个冰球棍，和家人在客厅里玩起了冰球游戏。

Joy tried to keep everyone's spirits up.

"I've got a great idea!" she yelled, **plugging** an idea bulb into the console.

Riley suddenly **grabbed** her hockey stick and the family played a goofy game of living room hockey.

就在这个时候，爸爸被叫去工作了，短暂的欢乐时光结束了。

"唉，他不再爱我们了。真是太伤心了。"忧忧说，"轮到我操控了，对吧？"**她一步步向控制台走去，乐乐拦住了她。**

"莱莉都还没有吃午饭呢！"乐乐冲忧忧大喊。

But the fun came to an end when Dad was called away for work.

"Oh, he doesn't love us anymore. That's sad," said Sadness. "I should drive, right?" **She stepped up to the console but Joy blocked her.**

"Riley hasn't had lunch!" Joy yelped.

18

莱莉和妈妈一起出去吃比萨，没想到这竟然变成了一场灾难。比萨上竟然有西蓝花！

这可吓坏了厌厌。"算了，我不管了。"厌厌说着，起身离开了。

怒怒也爆发了："恭喜你，旧金山，你可算是把比萨给毁了！"

Riley and Mom went out for pizza, but that was a **disaster**, too. The pizza had broccoli on it!

Disgust was horrified. "That's it. I'm done," she said, walking off.

Anger lost it. "Congratulations, San Francisco, you've ruined pizza!"

午餐过后，莱莉和妈妈一起步行回家。乐乐拿出了莱莉在来新家的路上产生的快乐记忆球，想让她开心一些。**可是忧忧碰到了记忆球，记忆球"唰"地一下变成了蓝色。**

"干得好，忧忧。"厌厌说，"这下只要莱莉想起和爸爸在一起的时光，她就会伤心了。干得真漂亮！"

乐乐警告忧忧别再碰其他的记忆球了，可忧忧就是管不住自己。她碰掉了放在核心记忆架上的一颗核心记忆球，**结果，莱莉的淘气岛顿时变暗了。**

幸好乐乐把核心记忆球重新放回了核心记忆架上，淘气岛才恢复了光亮。

As Riley and Mom walked back home, Joy tried to **cheer** Riley up with a happy memory from the road trip. **But Sadness touched the memory and turned it blue!**

"Good going, Sadness," said Disgust. "When Riley thinks of that moment with Dad, she's gonna feel sad. **Bravo**."

Joy told Sadness not to touch any more memories, but Sadness couldn't help herself. She knocked a **core** memory out of the core memory holder, **causing Goofball Island to go dark.**

Fortunately, Joy put it back and Goofball powered up again.

乐乐不得不让忧忧远离莱莉的记忆。她让忧忧去读大脑手册——**专门介绍大脑世界的指南。**"你这个幸运的小家伙，能读到这么酷的书！我要赶快去工作了，生活就是这么不公平。"乐乐说。

Joy had to keep Sadness away from all of Riley's memories, so she told her to read mind manuals, **the instructional guides to the Mind World.** "You lucky dog! You're reading these cool things. I gotta go work. Life is so unfair," said Joy.

cheer　　　　鼓励
bravo　　　　好极了
core　　　　　核心
fortunately　幸运的是
instructional 提供指导的

难点单词

21

这时候，其他的情绪小人也开始抱怨了。
"这次搬家太失败了。" 怒怒说。
乐乐想让大家用乐观的心态去对待这件事情，可是他们都不愿意。

Meanwhile, the other Emotions **complained**.
"This move has been a bust," said Anger.
Joy tried to get them to see the bright side, but they refused.

难 点 单 词

complained 抱怨
（complain 的过去式）
bust　　　　 弄坏
recalled　　 回想
（recall 的过去式）

那天晚上，莱莉的妈妈走进莱莉的卧室，情绪小人们都以为会听到更多的坏消息。可是恰恰相反，**妈妈夸奖了莱莉，说她是个乐观的好女孩。** 情绪小人们都惊呆了！

莱莉睡着后，乐乐让莱莉梦到了莱莉最喜欢的一段有关滑冰的记忆。

"别担心。"乐乐"滑"进了莱莉的记忆中。她对莱莉说："我相信明天一定会是美好的一天。我保证。"

When Riley's mom came into her bedroom that night, the Emotions expected more bad news. But instead, **Mom thanked Riley for being such a happy girl.** The Emotions were shocked!

Once Riley fell asleep, Joy **recalled** one of Riley's favorite skating memories for her to dream about.

"Don't you worry," Joy said to Riley as she skated in time to the memory. "I'm gonna make sure that tomorrow is another great day. I promise."

第二天早晨，乐乐已经做好了准备。"好啦，今天是开学第一天！"她说。乐乐给每个情绪小人都分派了任务——也包括忧忧。

"这是你的**忧伤圆圈**。你的任务就是让所有的小忧伤都好好地待在这个圆圈里。"乐乐说。

The next morning, Joy was **ready**. "Okay, first day of school!" she said. Joy gave everyone an **assignment**—including Sadness.

"This is **the Circle of Sadness**. Your job is to make sure that all the sadness stays inside of it," she said.

莱莉同爸爸妈妈道别后就向新学校出发了。直到此刻，一切都进行得很顺利。

Riley said good-bye to her parents, and then she was off to her new school. So far, the day was going great.

开始上课的时候，莱莉的老师问了莱莉一些关于明尼苏达州的事情。乐乐回忆起了一段快乐的时光，莱莉的脸上也出现了一丝笑容。"我们几乎每个周末都要去湖上玩耍。"可是她刚说完，就立刻变得忧伤起来。

原来忧忧又把一颗装满快乐的黄色记忆球变成了忧郁的蓝色！

莱莉在大家的面前哭了起来。 这也是蓝色核心记忆球第一次进入大脑总部！

At the beginning of class, Riley's teacher asked Riley about Minnesota. Joy recalled a happy memory and Riley smiled. "We go out on the lake almost every weekend," she said. Then, suddenly, she felt **gloomy**.

Sadness had made another happy memory sad!

Riley cried in front of everyone, and for the first time ever a blue core memory **rolled** into Headquarters!

27

乐乐想把新来的核心记忆球从真空管里拿出去。
"不要啊，乐乐。"忧忧上前阻止她。

Joy tried to get rid of the new core memory through a **vacuum tube.**

"Joy, no," said Sadness, stopping her.

两个人在争执的过程中一不小心撞到了核心记忆架，五颗核心记忆球滚落到了地上。所有的个性小岛瞬间变得漆黑一片！

　　更糟糕的是，强力真空管把忧忧、乐乐和记忆球都吸出了大脑总部。

As they **struggled**, they bumped into the holder, and the five core memories **spilled** out. All the personality islands went dark!

Then the powerful vacuum tube sucked Sadness, Joy, and the memories right out of Headquarters.

whooshed　飞快地移动
（whoosh 的过去式）
deposited　放置
（deposit 的过去式）
bin　　　箱子

难点单词

　　乐乐和忧忧误打误撞地跌进了心理世界中一个存放记忆球的箱子里。乐乐迅速拾起了五颗黄色核心记忆球。但是那颗蓝色核心记忆球不见了。

Joy and Sadness were **whooshed** into the Mind World, and **deposited** into a **bin** of memory spheres. Joy quickly gathered all five yellow core memories. The blue core memory was missing.

"咱们可以搞定的。"乐乐说，"咱们只要赶快回到大脑总部，把核心记忆球放到原来的位置，莱莉就能恢复正常了。"

她们跑到淘气岛，然后沿着光束桥往回走。

"We can fix this," said Joy. "We just have to get back to Headquarters, plug the core memories in, and Riley will be back to normal."

They ran to Goofball Island and then began to walk across the lightline.

这时候，还在大脑总部里的怒怒、厌厌和怕怕想要学着乐乐的样子去操作控制台。**可是他们把事情搞得一团糟。**

Inside Headquarters, Anger, Disgust, and Fear tried to run things like Joy. **They were failing miserably.**

miserably　糟糕地
scrambled　忙作一团
（scramble 的过去式）
figure out　搞清楚

难点单词

吃晚餐的时候，莱莉的父母发现她有点儿反常。爸爸妈妈大脑里的情绪小人已经乱作一团，他们想弄清楚莱莉究竟是怎么了。

At dinnertime, Riley's parents noticed she wasn't acting like herself. Inside Mom's and Dad's minds, their Emotions **scrambled** as they tried to **figure out** what was going on with Riley.

33

莱莉的爸爸妈妈问了她一些问题，可是莱莉显得越来越烦躁。这个时候，怒怒激动得就像要沸腾了一样。

怕怕让他冷静点儿，对他说："不，不，不，千万别这样，开心一点儿！"

可是怒怒猛地把他推到一边，自己进行操控。**很快，莱莉的坏情绪就爆发了。**

"闭嘴！"她大喊道。

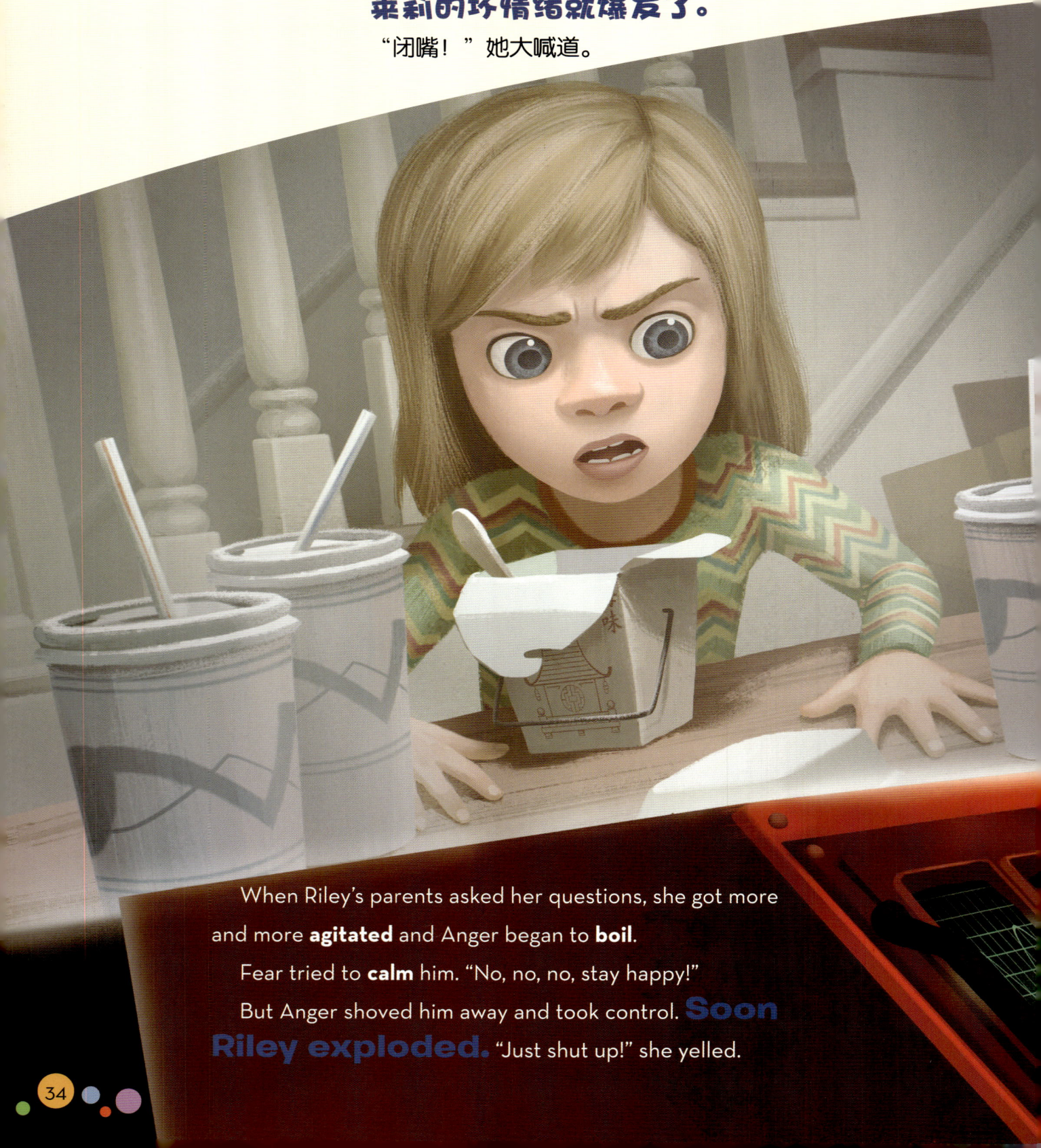

When Riley's parents asked her questions, she got more and more **agitated** and Anger began to **boil**.

Fear tried to **calm** him. "No, no, no, stay happy!"

But Anger shoved him away and took control. **Soon Riley exploded.** "Just shut up!" she yelled.

爸爸的情绪小人帮助他稳定住了情绪，**他让莱莉回到了自己的房间。**

Dad's Emotions helped him "put the foot down," and **Riley was sent to her room.**

apart　　　分开（的）
below　　　在……的下面
term　　　　期限
重点单词

晚上，虽然爸爸一直想要莱莉开心一点儿，莱莉却无动于衷。莱莉大脑中的淘气岛开始坍塌！

"快跑啊！"乐乐一边大喊，一边拉着忧忧沿着光束桥跑回地面，然后眼睁睁地看着**淘气岛崩塌并掉下深渊**。

Later that evening, Riley ignored her father's attempts to cheer her up, and Goofball Island started to fall **apart**!

"RUN!" yelled Joy. She and Sadness raced back across the lightline to solid ground just in time to watch **Goofball Island crumble into the abyss below**.

"我们只要绕路走就可以啦！"乐乐说。她拽着身后的忧忧，迈着大步，走向看不到尽头的**长期记忆储藏架**。

"We'll just have to go around!" said Joy. She marched toward the endless shelves of **Long Term Memory**, dragging Sadness behind her.

她们在迷宫一样的长期记忆储藏架之间绕了好几个小时。

不一会儿，她们发现了两个名叫**遗忘清洁员**的记忆清洁工。

They walked for **hours** through the **maze** of shelves in Long Term Memory.

Soon they spotted two Mind Workers called **Forgetters**.

他们的工作是把旧的记忆扔到**记忆填埋场**里去。

"一旦去了记忆填埋场，这些记忆就再也回不来了。"其中一个遗忘清洁员说。

Their job was to send old memories down to the **Memory Dump**.

"Nothing comes back from the dump," said one of the Forgetters.

这时候莱莉正抱着她的笔记本电脑，和她远在明尼苏达州的好朋友梅格聊天。当梅格提到一个新朋友时，怒怒再次掌管了控制台，于是莱莉"嘭"地一下关上了笔记本电脑。

友谊岛传来了低沉的破裂声。

Meanwhile, Riley was on her laptop computer, chatting with her best friend, Meg, in Minnesota. When Meg mentioned a new friend, Anger took over and Riley rudely **slammed** her laptop shut.

Friendship Island groaned!

当乐乐慌忙赶到的时候，她只能又一次眼睁睁地看着**友谊岛也沉入了记忆填埋场**。亲眼看到小岛落入黑暗之中，乐乐伤心极了。这种感觉就好像是弄丢了莱莉个性的一部分一样。

　　"唉，莱莉曾经多么珍爱友谊呀，可是现在它消失了。"忧忧说，"再见，友谊。你好，孤独。"

Joy ran to see **Friendship Island sink into the Memory Dump**. It was painful for Joy to **witness** the islands crumbling into the darkness. It was like losing parts of Riley's personality.

"Oh, Riley loved that one. And now it's gone," said Sadness. "Good-bye, friendship. Hello, loneliness."

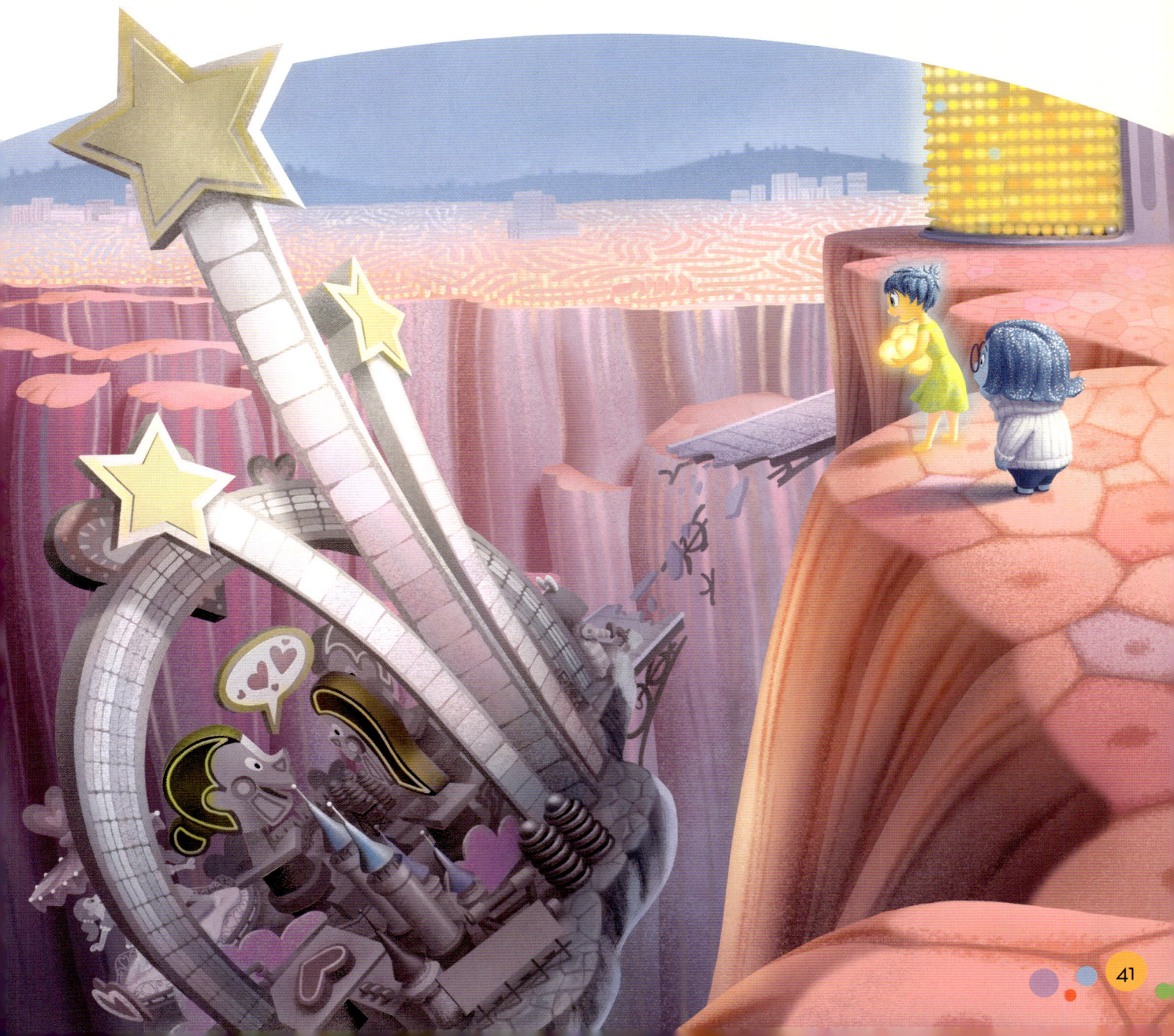

乐乐和忧忧继续在长期记忆区走啊走，终于遇见了一个熟悉的生物。**那是莱莉小时候想象出来的伙伴冰棒！** 他是用棉花糖做成的，长得有点儿像猫，有点儿像大象，又有点儿像海豚。莱莉三岁的时候，曾经和冰棒一起坐着他的音速战车火箭，经历了好几次冒险呢！

　　Joy and Sadness continued through Long Term Memory until they met up with a **familiar** creature. **It was Bing Bong, Riley's old imaginary friend!** He was part cat, part elephant, and part **dolphin**, and he was made of cotton candy. He and Riley had had many adventures in his song-powered **wagon** rocket when she was three.

冰棒建议大家乘坐**思想列车**去大脑总部。他还知道一条去车站的近路。

Bing Bong suggested they take the **Train of Thought** to Headquarters. He even knew a **shortcut** to the nearest station.

43

冰棒带着他们来到了一座名叫**抽象思维**的奇怪的大楼前。"车站到了。"他说。

"我在大脑手册里见过这个地方，我们不该进去。"忧忧赶忙拦住乐乐。

可是乐乐不想再浪费时间了。"我不会错过这趟列车的。"她一边说，一边快步跟在冰棒的后面。

Bing Borg led them to a **strange** building called **Abstract Thought**. "The **station** is right through here," he said.

"I read about this place in the manual. We shouldn't go in there," said Sadness.

But Joy didn't want to **waste** any more time. "I'm not missing that train," she said, hurrying after Bing Bong.

经过一番思想斗争，忧忧也跟了过去。

那天在学校里，莱莉一个人吃了午餐。她正在体验一种抽象思维：**孤独**。

Conflicted, Sadness followed.

At school that day, Riley ate lunch by herself. She was experiencing an **abstract** thought of her own: **loneliness**.

乐乐他们刚一迈进大楼，就听"嘭"的一声，大门关上了，屋子忽然变亮了。
"哦，不要啊，"忧忧喊道，"他们把开关打开了。"

Once they were inside the **building**, they heard the door slam and the room brightened. "Oh, no," cried Sadness. "They turned it on."

他们的身体开始扭曲成各种基本形状。

"我们变得抽象啦！"忧忧大喊。

他们一边继续变身，一边挣扎着跑到了屋子的另外一个出口前。然而，他们好不容易冲了出去，却发现列车刚刚开走。

Their bodies started to change into basic shapes.

"We're abstracting!" yelled Sadness.

As they continued to **transform**, they struggled toward the exit on the other side of the room. When they **finally** made it out, they saw the train leaving.

"那边还有一个车站，"冰棒指着**幻想乐园**说，"快点儿，咱们还能赶得上！"
冰棒激动地带着乐乐和忧忧在幻想乐园里转了一圈。

"There's another station," Bing Bong said, pointing toward **Imagination Land**.
"If we **hurry**, we can **catch** it!"
Bing Borg was thrilled to give Joy and Sadness a quick tour of Imagination Land.

hurry	快点
catch	赶上
favorite	最喜欢的

重点单词

　　冰棒带着他们走过奖杯小镇、薯条森林和乐乐最喜欢的云之城。这里还有一些连冰棒也没见过的新玩意儿，比如说梦幻男友制作器。

He took them to Trophy Town, French Fry Forest, and Cloud Town, which was Joy's **favorite**. There was even something new that Bing Bong hadn't seen before: an Imaginary Boyfriend Generator.

这时候，大脑总部里的三个情绪小人在为莱莉的冰球选拔赛做准备。

"如果她要使用冰球岛的话，冰球岛也会沉下去。"厌厌说。

"是啊，所以我已经把所有我能想起的冰球记忆都拿回来了。"怕怕说。

Inside Headquarters, the three Emotions prepared for Riley's hockey **tryouts**.

"If she tries to use Hockey Island, it's going down," said Disgust.

"Which is why I've recalled every hockey memory I can think of," said Fear.

怕怕把莱莉以前的冰球记忆一股脑儿塞进了核心记忆架，希望可以重新启动冰球岛。没想到，它们全都弹了回来。

"够了！让我来吧！"怒怒一把抢过控制台。

莱莉把球棍扔到一边，气冲冲地离开了冰球场。 冰球岛倒塌了！

He jammed old hockey memories into the core memory holder, hoping they would power the island, but they **shot** right out.

"That's it!" Anger yelled, taking control.

Riley threw her stick and stormed off the ice, causing Hockey Island to **collapse**!

pushed　　推
（push 的过去式）
chasing　　追逐
（chase 的现在分词形式）
believe　　相信

重点单词

乐乐想尽快赶到火车站，可就在这时，**冰棒看到自己的战车火箭快要被推下悬崖了**。

"别，别，不要啊！千万别把我的战车火箭扔到垃圾场去！我和莱莉还要坐着它飞去月球呢！"冰棒向着战车火箭的方向飞奔。可是已经来不及了，他的火箭掉下去了。

Joy wanted to hurry to the train station, **but Bing Bong saw his wagon rocket being pushed over the cliff.**

"No, no, no! You can't take my rocket to the dump! Riley and I are going to the moon!" said Bing Bong, **chasing** after it. But it was too late—his rocket was gone.

冰棒流下了糖果眼泪，忧忧赶忙过去安慰他。"你和莱莉一定经历过很棒的冒险。"她对冰棒说。

过了一会儿，冰棒擦干眼泪，说："我已经没事了。"

乐乐简直不敢相信，**忧忧竟然能让冰棒的心情好起来。**

Sadness comforted Bing Bong as he cried candy tears. "I bet you and Riley had great adventures," she told him.

After a while, Bing Bong wiped his eyes. "I'm okay now," he said. Joy couldn't **believe** it: **Sadness had actually helped him feel better.**

冰棒带着伙伴们及时赶到了火车站，大家都爬上了思想列车。但是没过多久，火车突然停了下来。"莱莉去睡觉了，"火车技师说，"我们也要休息了。"可是乐乐他们没办法等到天亮后火车继续开，因为那样就来不及了。这时候忧忧想到一个好主意："我们来把她叫醒怎么样？"

Bing Bong led them to the station just in time, and they all **climbed** aboard the Train of Thought. But it wasn't long before the train came to an abrupt stop. "Riley's gone to sleep," said the train engineer. "We're all on **break**." They couldn't wait until morning for the train to start running again! Sadness had an idea: "How about we **wake** her **up**?"

乐乐、忧忧和冰棒一路小跑来到了**造梦影城**。莱莉的梦就是在这里制造出来的。

Joy, Sadness, and Bing Bong **raced** to **Dream Productions**, where Riley's dreams were made.

"哇，这个地方好大啊。"乐乐怀着崇敬的心情环视四周。她还看到了她最喜欢的造梦明星——彩虹独角兽。

"Whoa! This place is **huge**," said Joy, looking around in **awe**.
She even spotted Rainbow Unicorn—her favorite dream star.

soundstage 摄影棚
rack 架子
sneaked 偷偷地走
（sneak 的过去式）
distortion 变形
filter 过滤器

难点单词

他们走进一扇摄影棚的大门，里面舞台上的布景很像莱莉的教室。他们躲在服装架后面，想出了一个主意。**忧忧想到一个可怕的梦可以吓醒莱莉**。但是乐乐不同意这么做。

They entered a **soundstage** door and saw a set that looked like Riley's classroom. They ducked behind a costume **rack** and came up with a plan. **Sadness thought a scary dream would wake Riley**, but Joy didn't want that.

58

乐乐说："我们要让她快乐地醒过来！"乐乐找到了一套小狗服装。她和忧忧套上这套服装，溜到了舞台上。

梦境导演告诉摄影师加上一些现实再现滤镜。摄影师换上一个特殊的镜头，这时候，造梦影城的演员们看上去就像是莱莉的老师和同学！

"We'll excite her awake!" she said. Joy found a dog costume and handed half to Sadness. Then the two of them **sneaked** onto the set.

The dream director told the cameraman to add the reality-**distortion filter**. He slipped the special lens on the camera, and the Dream Productions cast suddenly looked like Riley's teacher and classmates!

在大脑总部里，轮到怕怕值班盯着莱莉的梦境。他在屏幕前看到那只小狗在上蹿下跳。

突然，道具服裂开了，屏幕上出现了乐乐和忧忧的身影。但是通过现实再现滤镜，小狗就好像从中间被劈成了两半一样！

"这只是一个梦，只是一个梦，只是一个梦……"怕怕一遍一遍地对自己说。

忧忧的主意起作用了：**他们正在一点点地把莱莉吓醒！**

Fear was on Dream Duty in Headquarters, so he watched as the dog **pranced** onto the screen. The costume suddenly ripped, revealing Joy and Sadness. But through the reality-distortion filter, it looked like the dog had **split** in half!

"It's just a dream, it's just a dream, it's just a dream . . ." Fear chanted.

Sadness's plan was working: **they were scaring Riley awake!**

但是梦境导演发现了舞台上的不速之客，她立刻喊来了保安。乐乐和忧忧逃了出来，冰棒却被抓走了！

But then the director spotted the **intruders** on the set and called security. Joy and Sadness managed to **escape**, but Bing Bong was taken away!

balloon	气球
horrific	可怕的
clown	小丑
belly	腹部

难点单词

保安一路把冰棒拖到了潜意识里。在那扇门后面，锁着莱莉最阴暗的恐惧。

The guards dragged Bing Bong down to the Subconscious, where all of Riley's darkest fears were kept behind locked doors.

62

乐乐和忧忧溜了进去。他们避开了祖母的真空吸尘器和通往地下室的台阶，来到可怕的小丑叮当面前，发现冰棒就被关在小丑身上的气球笼子里。乐乐悄悄地爬到小丑的肚子上，救出了冰棒。

　　Joy and Sadness sneaked inside. They avoided Grandma's vacuum cleaner and the stairs to the basement, and found Bing Bong inside a **balloon** cage on top of a **horrific clown** named Jangles! Joy quietly climbed up the clown's **belly** and freed Bing Bong.

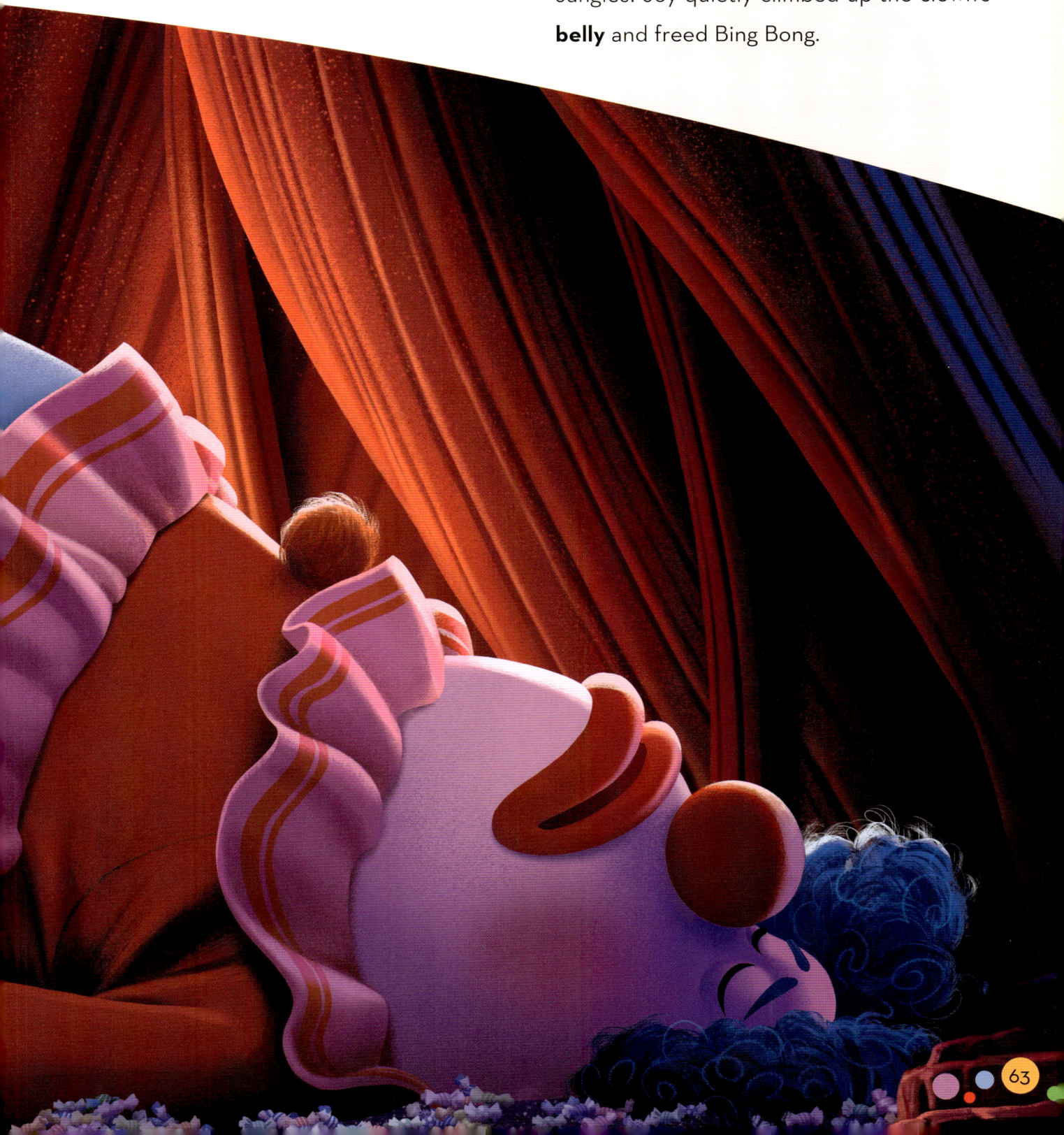

看着小丑叮当，乐乐和忧忧想到了一个叫醒莱莉的好办法。她们按了按小丑巨大的鼻子，把叮当弄醒了，然后引着他一路来到了造梦影城！

Looking at Jangles, Joy and Sadness knew what they had to do to wake up Riley. They honked the **giant** clown's nose to wake him and led him **straight** to Dream Productions!

小丑叮当突然袭击了摄影棚，冰棒、忧忧和乐乐迅速地跑到思想列车前跳了上去。

可怕的噩梦把莱莉吓醒了。这时候，火车开始缓缓前进！

As Jangles stormed **through** the soundstage, Bing Bong, Sadness, and Joy ran to the Train of Thought and hopped on.

The intense nightmare jolted Riley awake and the train started to ran!

awful　　　　糟糕的
discovered　发现
（discover 的过去式）
positive　　　积极的

重点单词

在大脑总部里，**怒怒想到了一个主意。** 自从来到旧金山，一切都变得糟糕起来，所以他觉得莱莉应该回到明尼苏达州去。"你们同意吗？"他问。

厌厌和怕怕都点头同意了。怒怒把一个灵光一现球塞进了控制台。

Back inside Headquarters, **Anger had an idea.** Since everything turned **awful** after they arrived in San Francisco, he thought Riley should run away back to Minnesota. "Who's with me?" he asked.

Disgust and Fear agreed, and Anger plugged an idea bulb into the console.

在火车上，乐乐和忧忧发现，**她们最喜欢的一段记忆是相同的。**

"哈，小姑娘！你也开朗起来了！"乐乐说。

忧忧盯着眼前的记忆球，回忆起莱莉输掉冰球季后赛的事。莱莉错过了制胜的一击。

乐乐叹了口气，忧忧记得的事情总是和乐乐的不一样。乐乐答应忧忧等回到大脑总部以后，就帮忧忧变得积极向上起来。

On the train, Joy and Sadness **discovered** they shared the same favorite memory.

"Atta girl! Now you're getting it!" said Joy.

Sadness stared at the memory, recalling the moment when Riley's hockey team had lost the big playoff game. Riley had missed the winning shot.

Joy sighed. Sadness had remembered it all wrong. Joy promised to help Sadness work on her **positive** outlook when they got back to Headquarters.

这时候，莱莉已经准备好要离家出走了。她偷了妈妈的信用卡去买公共汽车票。**诚实岛轰然倒塌**，思想列车的轨道也随之断裂。

工人们赶在火车**掉进垃圾场**之前，把乐乐、忧忧和冰棒拉了出来。"我们又少了一座小岛。到底发生了什么事情？"乐乐大喊。

"你们没有听说吗？"一个记忆清洁工说，"莱莉离家出走了。"

Meanwhile, Riley was getting ready to run away from home. When she stole her mom's credit card to buy a bus ticket, **Honesty Island crumbled** and caused the Train of Thought tracks to collapse.

Workers rushed to help Joy, Sadness, and Bing Bong off the train before it **fell into the dump!** "We lost another island. What is happening?" Joy cried.

"Haven't you heard?" said a Mind Worker. "Riley is running away."

| beneath | 下面 |
| nearby | 附近的 |

难 点 单 词

莱莉离开家，向着汽车站的方向走去。**家庭岛开始崩塌了。**这时候，一些长期记忆储藏架也纷纷断裂了，露出一条记忆召回管道。记忆召回管道把记忆球重新召回了大脑总部。

"我们也可以被召回总部！"忧忧激动起来。

但是乐乐不想让忧忧碰到记忆球，那样记忆球就会变成忧伤的蓝色。她只好自己一个人进入了管道。可她还没有前进多远，管道就突然断裂了，**乐乐和所有的记忆球都掉了下来！**

冰棒伸出手去抓乐乐，但他脚下的地面也塌了。忧忧只能站在一旁的悬崖上，眼看着乐乐和冰棒跌进了记忆填埋场里。

As Riley left her house and began walking to the bus station, **Family Island began to crumble.** Then some of the shelves in Long Term Memory broke open, exposing a recall tube. Recall tubes sent memory spheres back up to Headquarters.

"We can get recalled!" Sadness said.

But Joy didn't want Sadness to turn the core memories blue, so she rode up the tube alone. She didn't get far. The tube broke open and **Joy and all the core memories fell out!**

As Bing Bong reached out to grab Joy, the ground **beneath** him gave way. Sadness watched from a **nearby** cliff as Joy and Bing Bong fell into the Memory Dump.

乐乐绝望了。她觉得自己辜负了莱莉。这时候，她找到了她和忧忧在思想列车上聊起的记忆球。

　　注视着这段记忆，她突然意识到了什么。在这段记忆里，莱莉最快乐的时光，是在沮丧的时候，父母和队友一起为她加油鼓劲。乐乐终于明白：**离开忧忧，莱莉是不会开心起来的。**

　　"我们必须赶紧回去！"乐乐对冰棒说。

Joy was **devastated**. She thought she had failed Riley. She found the memory sphere she and Sadness had talked about on the Train of Thought.

As she watched the memory, she realized something. The **joyful** part of the memory, when Riley's parents and **teammates** had come to cheer her up, had happened because Riley had felt sad. Joy finally understood: **Riley couldn't be happy without Sadness.**

"We have to get back up there!" Joy said to Bing Bong.

71

突然，乐乐想到了一个好主意！她和冰棒可以乘坐战车火箭冲出记忆填埋场！

Suddenly, Joy had an idea! She and Bing Bong could ride his wagon rocket out of the Memory Dump!

他们从碎石堆里找到战车火箭并跳了进去。接着，他们在战车火箭里大声唱歌。**战车火箭腾空而起，冲向上方的悬崖。** 乐乐已经可以碰到悬崖壁了，可是他们离顶端还远着呢！

他们试了一次又一次，可是高度总也不够，无法飞出垃圾场。

They found the rocket among the **rubble** and hopped in. Then they began to sing as loudly as they could. **The rocket soared toward the cliffs above.** Joy reached for the **ledge**, but they weren't even close.

They tried again and again but could never get high enough to escape the dump.

fade　　　　逐渐消失
feeling　　　感觉
jumped　　　跳
（jump 的过去式）

重点单词

冰棒注意到**自己正在渐渐地消失**。"加油，乐乐，我们再试一次。我有预感，这次一定能成功。"

Bing Bong noticed **he was starting to fade.**
"Come on, Joy, one more time. I've got a **feeling** about this one."

趁乐乐一不留神，冰棒从车上跳了出去。战车火箭越飞越高……终于越过了悬崖！

"太棒了！冰棒，我们成功了！我们……"乐乐俯身看到冰棒正在悬崖下面欢呼。

"哈哈哈，你成功了！快去拯救莱莉吧！带她去月球玩，好吗？"冰棒向乐乐**挥了挥手，消失了。**

Without Joy's noticing, he **jumped** out. The rocket soared higher and higher . . . and made it over the ledge!

"Woo-hoo! Bing Bong, we did it! We—" Joy looked down to see Bing Bong cheering below.

"Ha, ha, ha! You made it! Go save Riley! Take her to the moon for me, okay?" **Then he waved and faded away.**

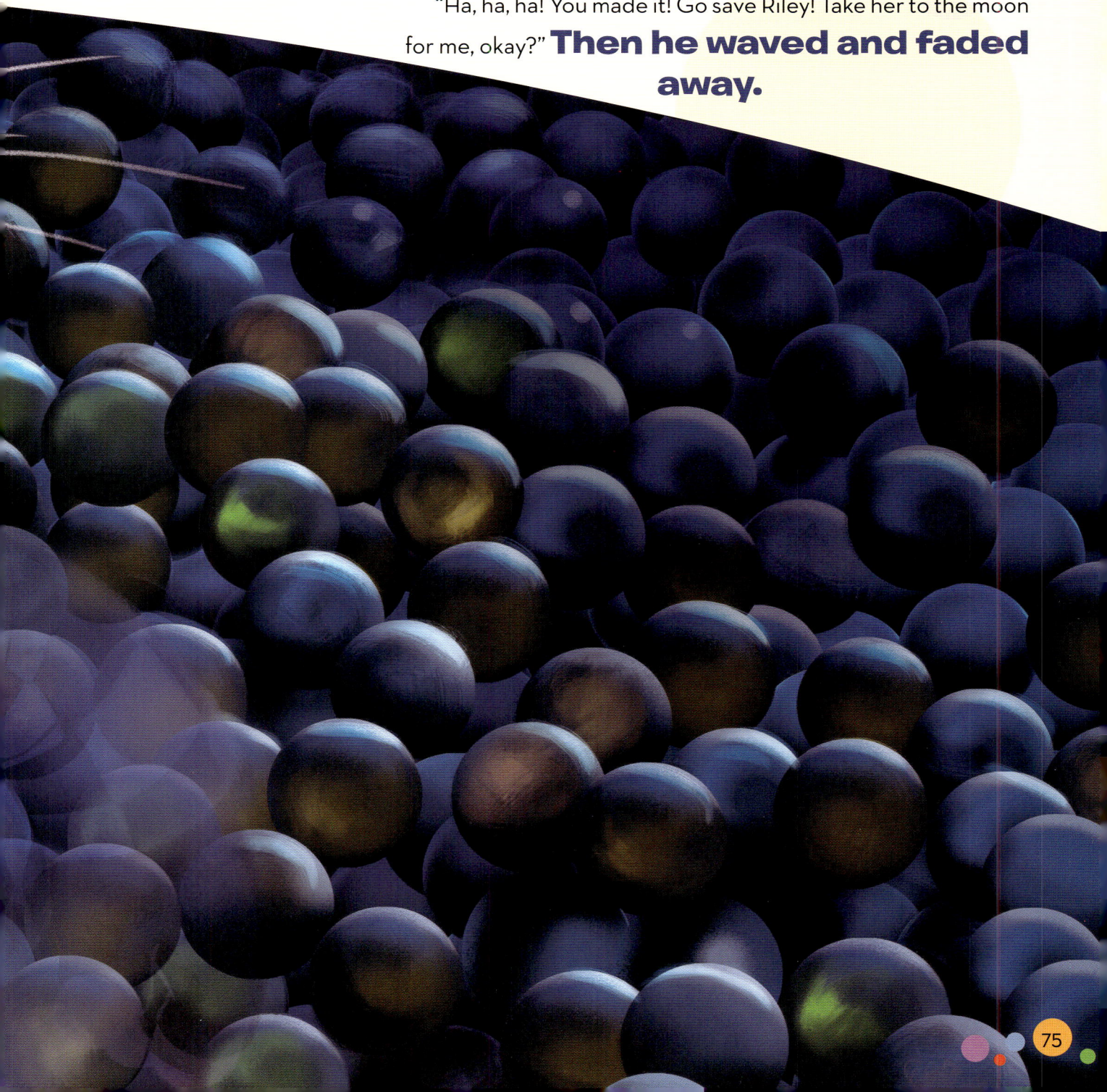

surprised　　惊奇
（surprise 的过去式）
pick up　　捡起
remove　　去除
panic　　恐慌

重点单词

　　莱莉的爸爸妈妈回家后，发现莱莉没有从学校回来，他们惊讶极了。他们试着打她的手机，可是莱莉没有接电话。

When Riley's parents got home, they were **surprised** to see she wasn't back from school. They tried calling her cell phone, but she didn't **pick up**.

在大脑总部里，怒怒、怕怕和厌厌都对离家计划后悔不已。

"太疯狂了！"怒怒大吼，"**她不应该逃跑的！**"

"咱们来把这个主意从她的大脑里清除掉吧。"厌厌说。

他们想把灵光一现球拿走，可是它就是一动也不动。大家陷入了一团慌乱中，发疯般地狂按控制台上的每一个按钮！

In Headquarters, Anger, Fear, and Disgust were regretting the plan.

"This is madness!" shouted Anger. **"She shouldn't run away!"**

"Let's get that idea out of her head," said Disgust.

They tried to **remove** the idea bulb, but it wouldn't move. Then they started to **panic** and pushed every button on the console!

乐乐追着忧忧，一路从长期记忆储藏架跑到了幻想乐园。"莱莉没有我会更好！"忧忧伤心地喊着。她跳上了一朵云彩，随风飘走了。

　　这时候，乐乐想到了一个疯狂的主意。**她用幻想男友制造器造出了好多男友，并让他们叠起了罗汉。**

　　"发射！"乐乐一声令下，所有的幻想男友都向前倾倒，把乐乐发射到了即将崩塌的家庭岛的蹦床上。在蹦床上弹了一下后，乐乐再次飞向空中，直奔忧忧的方向而去。

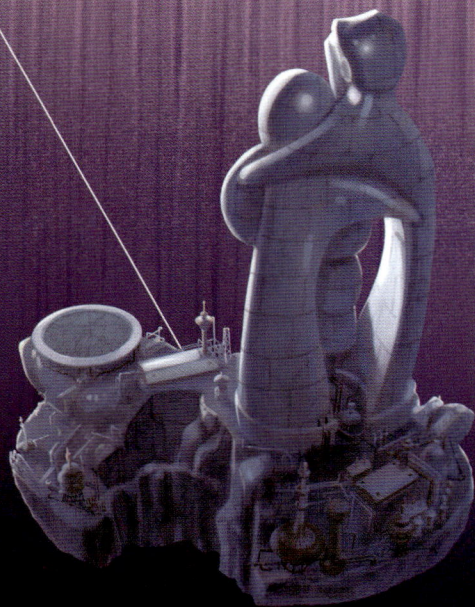

Joy chased Sadness through Long Term Memory and into Imagination Land. "Riley's better off without me!" she yelled as she hopped onto a cloud and flied away.

Then Joy had a crazy idea. **She used the Imaginary Boyfriend Generator to create a tower of boyfriends.**

"NOW!" she yelled. All the imaginary boyfriends leaned forward and launched Joy onto a **trampoline** on the crumbling Family Island. She **bounced** off it and **zoomed** into the air, right toward Sadness.

trampoline　蹦床
bounced　弹跳
（bounce 的过去式）
zoomed　急速上升
（zoom 的过去式）

难点单词

grabbed　　抓住
（grab 的过去式）
brilliant　　极好的
inside　　　里面

重点单词

"抓紧啦！" 乐乐一把抓住忧忧。两个情绪小人一起飞向大脑总部，一头撞到了窗户上。

　　怒怒、厌厌和怕怕看到她们的时候都激动极了。现在只剩下一个问题：他们无法打开大脑总部的窗户。

"Hang on!" Joy yelled as she **grabbed** Sadness. The two soared toward Headquarters and hit right into the window!

Anger, Disgust, and Fear were thrilled to see them. There was just one problem: the windows in Headquarters didn't open.

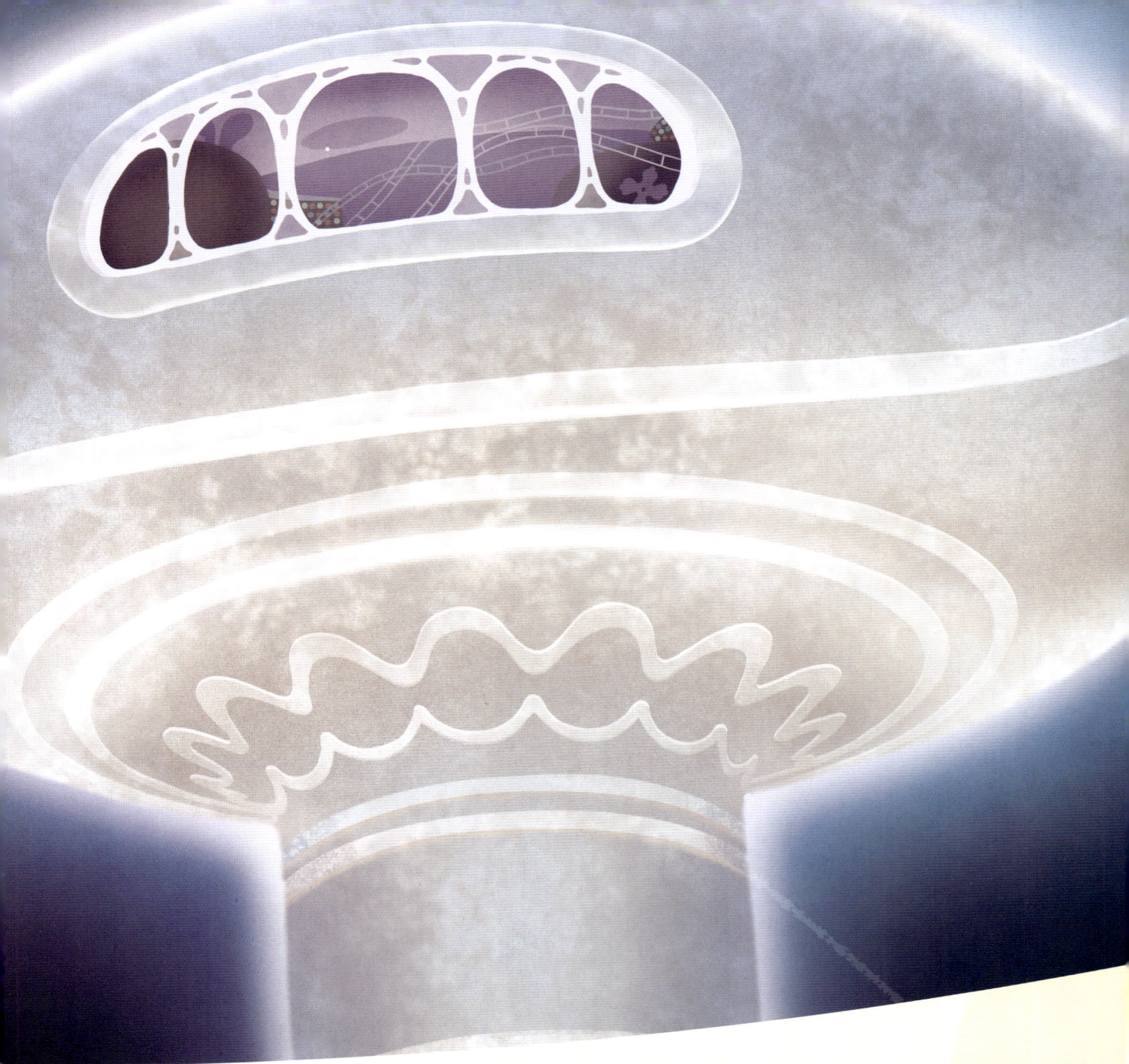

厌厌想到了一个绝妙的主意。**她先惹怒怒怒生气，然后用怒怒头上的火焰烧穿了玻璃。** 乐乐和忧忧终于爬进来了。

Disgust had a **brilliant** idea. **She made Anger mad and used the flames from his head to cut through the glass.** Joy and Sadness climbed **inside**.

"忧忧，就看你的啦。"乐乐说，"莱莉需要你。"

在情绪小人们的注视下，忧忧一步一步地走向控制台，轻轻地拿出灵光一现球。

这时候，莱莉正在公共汽车上。她突然站了起来，说："我要下车。"然后，她冲下车，头也不回地跑回了家。

"Sadness, it's up to you," said Joy. "Riley needs you."

The Emotions watched as Sadness stepped up to the console and gently pulled the idea bulb out.

Inside the bus, Riley stood up. "I wanna get off, " she said, and ran home.

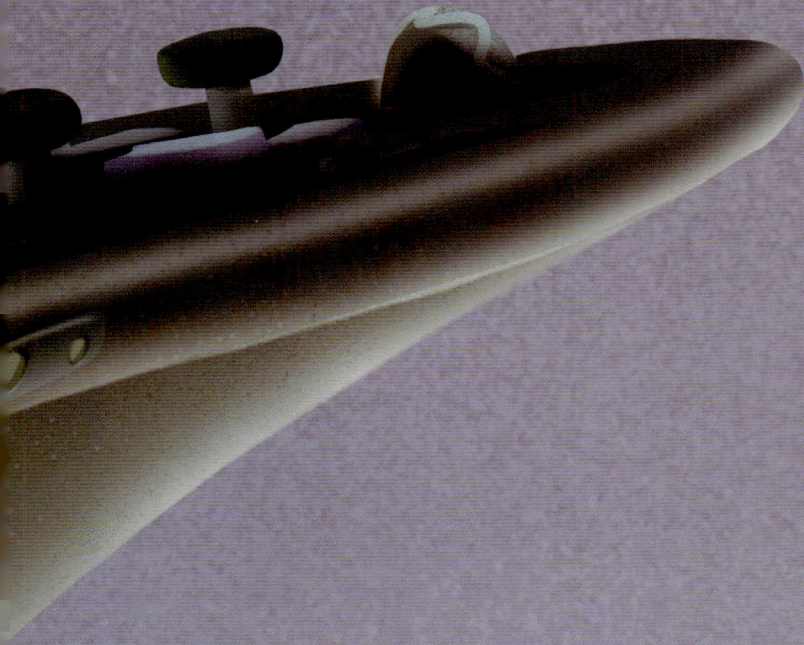

莱莉推开家门走了进去，爸爸妈妈总算松了口气。在大脑总部里，**乐乐递给忧忧五颗核心记忆球**。顿时，五颗核心记忆球都变成了蓝色。忧忧把它们放进记忆召回装置里，记忆球开始在莱莉的大脑中运转。

　　莱莉大哭了起来。

Riley's parents were relieved when she walked through the front door. In Headquarters, **Joy handed the five core memories to Sadness**, and each one turned blue. Sadness placed them in the recall **unit** and they played through Riley's mind.

　　Riley began to cry.

"我知道你们不想让我这样，可……我想家了。我想明尼苏达州了。"莱莉抽泣着说。

妈妈和爸爸对莱莉说，他们也想明尼苏达州了。**三个人拥抱在一起，莱莉终于破涕为笑。**

这时，一颗新的核心记忆球滚进了大脑总部。这颗核心记忆球是由蓝色和黄色两种颜色混合在一起的。当这颗记忆球滚入核心记忆架上时，一个新的家庭岛诞生了。

"I know you don't want me to, but . . . I **miss** home. I miss Minnesota," Riley said.

Mom and Dad told her they missed Minnesota, too. **The three of them embraced, and Riley smiled through her tears.**

At that moment, a new core memory rolled into Headquarters. It was blue and yellow—all swirled together. The sphere settled into the core memory holder and generated a brand-new Family Island.

在之后的几个月里，莱莉的生活和她的大脑世界都发生了许多积极的变化。看到一座座**新出现的个性小岛**，情绪小人们激动万分。

"我爱吸血鬼悲剧爱情岛。"忧忧说。

In the following months, there were a lot of good changes both in Riley's world and in her Mind World. The Emotions were **excited** about the **new Islands of Personality** that had **formed**.

"I like Tragic Vampire Romance Island," said Sadness.

"男孩乐队岛，希望这只是一个短暂的阶段。"怕怕说。

不仅如此，情绪小人们在大脑总部里的控制台也升级了。

"嘿，大伙儿说说，什么是青——春——期？"厌厌问道，她发现了一个大大的红色按钮。

"Boy Band Island. Hope that's just a phase," said Fear.

The Emotions also got an upgraded console installed in Headquarters.

"Hey, guys, what's pub-er-ty?"asked Disgust, as she **inspected** a large, red button.

bleachers　　露天看台
embarrassed　尴尬的
awesome　　令人赞叹的

难点单词

　　莱莉加入了一支旧金山的冰球队，在那里她认识了很多超棒的新朋友。

　　比赛的时候，莱莉的爸爸妈妈坐在看台上，为莱莉加油助威。

　　"加油，雾角队！"爸爸大喊着。

　　"加油，莱莉！"妈妈欢呼着。

Riley hac joined a San Francisco hockey team and made some great new friends.

During one of the games, Riley's parents sat in the **bleachers**, cheering her on.

"GO, FOGHORNS!" shouted Dad.

"GO, RILEY!" exclaimed Mom.

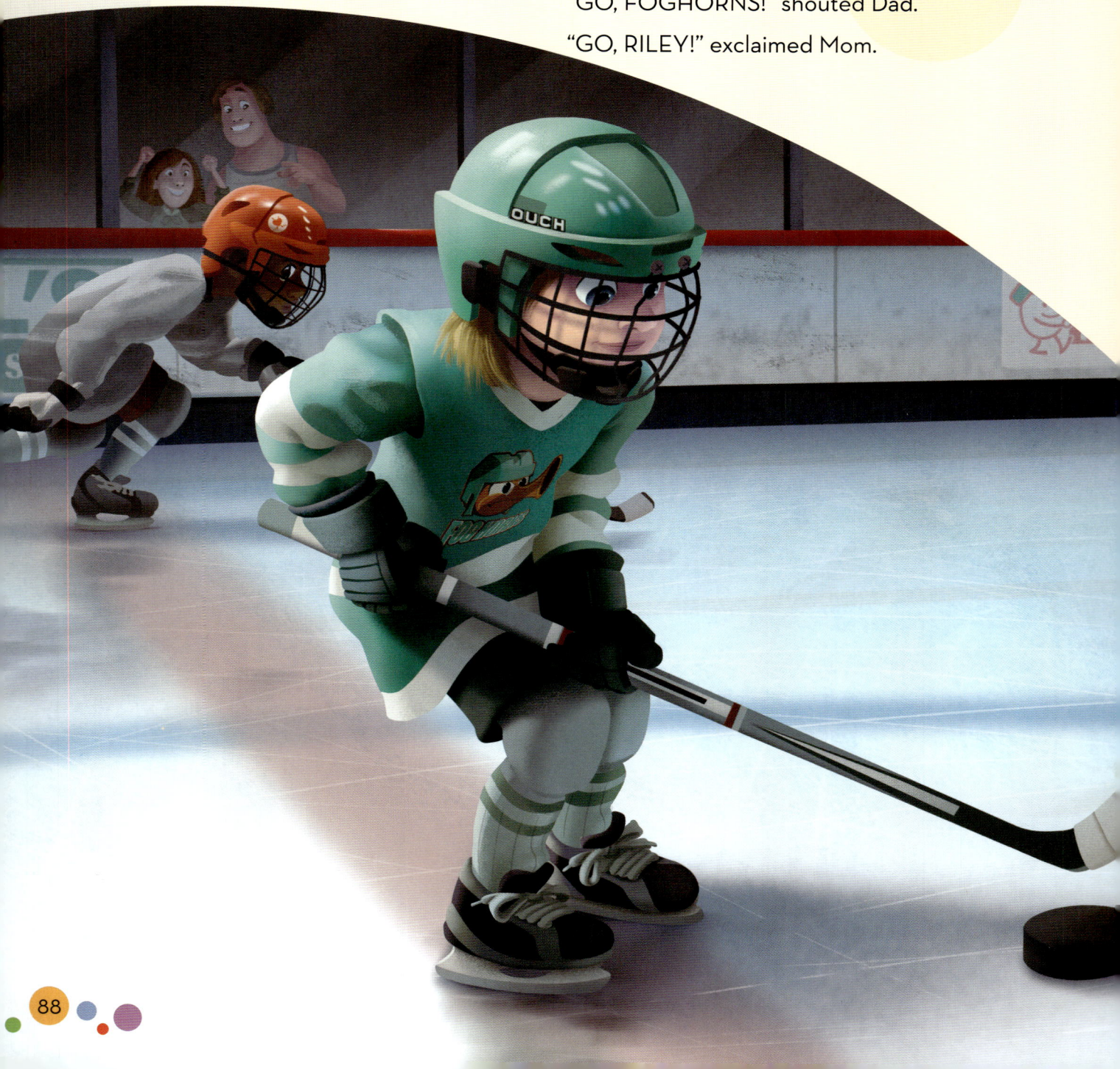

莱莉觉得有点儿尴尬，可她必须承认，**爸爸妈妈太棒了**。她滑进冰球场，准备开始比赛。情绪小人们也都准备就绪了。

"好了，"乐乐说，"我们来打冰球吧！"

Riley felt a little **embarrassed**, but she had to admit—**Mom and Dad were pretty awesome**.

She skated onto the ice, ready to play, as the Emotions prepared.

"All right," said Joy. "Let's play some hockey!"

乐乐和忧忧并排站在控制台前。她们知道，**只有团队协作才能帮助莱莉幸福地生活。**

对于莱莉来说，现在的一切都棒极了。她认识了很棒的新朋友，加入了新的冰球队，住进了新的房子，而且她已经十二岁了。还能有什么让她不开心的事儿呢？

Joy and Sadness stood side by side at the console. They knew that **working together as a team was the best way to help Riley lead a happy life.**

And right now, things were great for Riley. She had **fantastic** new friends, a new hockey team, a new house, and she had turned twelve years old. What could **possibly** go wrong?

A

abstract	抽象的
apart	分开（的）
assignment	任务
awe	崇敬
awful	糟糕的

B

believe	相信
below	在……的下面
break	中间休息
brilliant	极好的
building	楼房

C

catch	赶上
center	中心
challenges	挑战

（challenge 的复数形式）

chasing	追逐

（chase 的现在分词形式）

circle	圆圈
climbed	爬

（climb 的过去式）

conflicted	感到矛盾
control panel	控制台

D

disaster	灾难
discovered	发现

（discover 的过去式）

dolphin	海豚
dump	垃圾场

E

embraced	拥抱

（embrace 的过去式）

excited	兴奋的

F

fade	逐渐消失
familiar	熟悉的
family	家庭
fantastic	极好的
favorite	最喜欢的
feeling	感觉
finally	终于
formed	形成

（form 的过去式）

G

gently	轻轻地
giant	巨大的
grabbed	抓住

（grab 的过去式）

H

hours	小时

（hour 的复数形式）

huge	巨大的
hurry	快点儿

I

in charge	负责

inside　　　里面
inspected　　　检查
（inspect 的过去式）

J

joy　　　欢乐
jumped　　　跳
（jump 的过去式）

M

maze　　　迷宫
miss　　　想念

N

nightmare　　　噩梦

P

panic　　　恐慌
pick up　　　捡起
planned　　　计划
（plan 的过去式）
positive　　　积极的
possibly　　　可能地
pulled　　　拉，扯
（pull 的过去式）
pushed　　　推
（push 的过去式）

R

raced　　　跑
（race 的过去式）
ready　　　准备好的
remove　　　去除

S

screen　　　屏幕
shortcut　　　近路
slammed　　　猛地关上
（slam 的过去式）
station　　　车站
stepped　　　行走
（step 的过去式）
straight　　　直接地
strange　　　奇怪的
surprised　　　惊奇
（surprise 的过去式）

T

tasks　　　任务
（task 的复数形式）
term　　　期限
through　　　穿过
together　　　在一起
transform　　　变换

U

unit　　　单元
upgraded　　　升级的

W

wagon　　　四轮运货车
wake up　　　叫醒
waste　　　浪费
witness　　　见证
wonder　　　惊奇

多样的情绪

头脑特工队里有五个情绪小人，把情绪小人的图片与他们的名字以及代表他们所发挥的作用的图片连起来吧！

Joy

Sadness

Fear

Disgust

Anger

情绪小人们在莱莉的大脑世界里经历了什么？选择合适的单词来描述下面图片的内容吧！

1. we are_____.

    A. happy   B. sad

2. we are_____.

    A. walking   B. running

3. I feel_____.

    A. angry   B. embarrassed

4. I am_____.

    A. reading   B. playing

5. It is a_____ball.

    A. yellow   B. blue

答案：1-5：ABAAA

忧忧不小心把下面单词里字母的顺序打乱了，这可忙坏了情绪小人们。快来帮他们一起写出正确的单词吧！如果实在想不出来，可以参考后面的中文意思。

SEMEOAW　　＿＿＿＿＿＿＿＿　极好的

NECGAH　　＿＿＿＿＿＿＿＿　改变

FOMCORT　　＿＿＿＿＿＿＿＿　安慰

IOEGRN　　＿＿＿＿＿＿＿＿　忽视

TOEFN　　＿＿＿＿＿＿＿＿　经常

OPELBMR　　＿＿＿＿＿＿＿＿　问题

TATSNOI　　＿＿＿＿＿＿＿＿　车站

OGHUTRH　　＿＿＿＿＿＿＿＿　穿过

答案：1.awesome 2.change 3.comfort 4.ignore 5.often 6.problem 7.station 8.through

95

一起来完成更有挑战性的句子吧！把正确的单词填在下面句子里的横线上。

moved

guide

turned

1. Fear can safely _____ her to the other side.

2. They _____ the family to San Francisco.

3. Sadness touched the memory and _____ it blue.

4. They are _____ about their favorite memories.

5. Her parents asked her some _____ .

questions

talking